THE ZACK FILES

Hang a Left at Venus

For Judith, and for the real Zack,
with love—D.G.

THE ZACK FILES™

Hang a Left at Venus

By Dan Greenburg

Illustrated by Jack E. Davis

SCHOLASTIC INC.

New York Toronto London Auckland Sydney
Mexico City New Delhi Hong Kong

I'd like to thank my editor
Jane O'Connor who makes the process
of writing and revising so much fun,
and without whom
these books would not exist.

I also want to thank Catherine Daly,
Laura Driscoll, and Emily Neye
for their terrific ideas.

ISBN 0-439-28528-3

12 11 10 9 8 7 6 5 4 3 2   1 2 3 4 5 6/0

Printed in the U.S.A.   40

First Scholastic printing, February 2001

Chapter 1

I've always thought about being abducted by creatures from another planet. But when I finally came face-to-face with a real-life alien, I was the one doing the abducting! But I think I'm getting ahead of my story. First I should tell you who I am and stuff.

My name is Zack, and I'm ten and a half. I go to the Horace Hyde-White School for Boys. That's in New York. My parents are divorced, and I spend half my time with each of them. I was with my dad the night this UFO thing started.

Dad and I had just left a movie in Central Park. I know it sounds weird, but sometimes they show movies at night in the park. It's sort of like a drive-in without the cars. And all around you are the twinkling lights of New York City skyscrapers. It's really cool.

Anyway, Dad and I were walking through the park to get a cab. Usually, walking through the park at night is a stupid thing to do. But there were lots of people from my school in the park. Plus, I was with my dad, so I wasn't afraid.

My dad is pretty brave. He's also very strong. He's a writer. I don't know if writing is what makes him strong. I do know he has these very strong fingers from typing, though. He could squeeze your arm or your nose pretty hard if he wanted to.

We were walking up this path toward Fifth Avenue to get a cab. We passed by two people in trench coats. A man and a woman. They were holding flashlights and poking around in the bushes. The woman had reddish hair. The man had brown hair and a very worried expression. Dad and I shrugged and kept walking.

Then, just past this really tall hedge, I saw a weird glow.

"Hey, Dad," I said. "What's that weird glow up ahead?"

"Probably the light from one of the park lampposts," he said.

"No," I said. "It's a different kind of light than that. It's an eerie glow."

"Well, we'll see what kind of glow it is when we get there," said Dad.

As soon as we got there, I saw what the glow was coming from. It wasn't coming from a lamppost. It was coming from a large silver something. It was shaped kind of like a Frisbee. Round, but with a dome in the middle. It was about the size of a Honda Civic. It was floating about three feet off the ground. And it was glowing. Eerily. There was a little rope ladder hanging off the edge of it.

"Dad," I whispered. "What the heck is *that*?"

Dad looked really surprised. He just stared at the glowing thing and shook his head.

"I don't know, Zack," he whispered.

"Is it a UFO?" I whispered.

"Uh, oh no, no," he whispered. "Nothing like that. I'm sure it's something much more ordinary than that."

"Then what is it?"

"Well, just now it's hard to say," he whispered. "It may be a new kind of park vehicle. It's not a UFO, though."

"Then why are you whispering?"

"Uh, I usually whisper when I discover things that look like UFO's but aren't," he said.

Just then we heard a noise in the bushes. Next thing we knew, this kid came out of the bushes. At least I thought it was a kid. It was kid-sized. But when it caught sight of us, it let out a little scream. Then it fell over. I think it fainted.

"Yikes!" I whispered. "What the heck is *that*?"

"Uh, probably a child," said Dad. "A boy from your school who went to the movie."

We crept a little closer.

"A boy wearing a tin-foil suit?" I said.

"Possibly," said Dad.

We crept a little closer.

"A boy with no hair, no ears, and a weird nose?" I said.

"Possibly," said Dad.

"I don't know any boys at school who wear tin-foil suits," I said. "Or boys who have no hair, no ears, and weird noses."

"Maybe it's...a boy you don't know," said Dad.

"I think it's a creature from another planet," I said.

"We don't have any reason to believe that," said Dad.

"What do you think's wrong with him?" I said. "Do you think he fainted?"

"Probably," said Dad. He reached out and took the creature's wrist.

"What are you doing?" I said. I thought he was pretty brave even to be touching it. I told you my dad was brave.

"I'm trying to see if he has a pulse," said Dad. "Oh, good. He's got one."

Dad held the creature's wrist and looked at his watch.

"Normal pulse is about seventy-two,"

said Dad. "Your pulse goes up if you have a fever. Down if you're asleep or unconscious."

"What's this guy's pulse?" I asked.

"Three hundred forty-seven," said Dad.

"So that means...?" I said.

"Either he has a really high fever or he's a creature from another planet," said Dad.

Chapter 2

"So, Dad," I said. "At least you admit this is a creature from another planet."

"Or else a boy with a really high fever," said Dad.

"Have you ever heard of anybody who had a pulse of three hundred forty-seven?" I asked.

"Not really," said Dad. "Well, whatever he is, I think we have to revive him somehow."

"How about mouth-to-mouth?" I suggested.

"I don't think so," said Dad. "To tell you the truth, I'm not even sure which opening is the mouth."

"How about giving him the old Heimlich maneuver?" I suggested. "You did that to me in that movie theater when I was choking on popcorn. Remember? You hug somebody from behind and squeeze."

"The Heimlich maneuver is used if you get a piece of steak or popcorn stuck in your throat," said Dad. "I didn't see him chewing steak or popcorn. Who knows what's wrong with him. I think we have to get him to a doctor, Zack. As soon as possible. I'll call Dr. Kropotkin from a pay phone."

Dad bent down and picked the creature up. We walked away from the UFO and headed toward Fifth Avenue. Dad found a pay phone and called. Even though it was late, Dr. Kropotkin said to come straight to his home.

A cab stopped on Fifth Avenue. We got in. Dad lay the creature in the tin-foil suit down on the seat.

Dad gave the driver Dr. Kropotkin's home address.

The cab started forward. I could see the driver studying us in his rear-view mirror.

"What you got there, a sick kid?" the driver asked.

"Actually, we think it's a creature from outer space," I said.

"That right?" said the driver. "How about that. You know, I had a creature from outer space in my cab once."

"Really?" I said. "Where did you take him?"

"Bloomingdale's," said the driver.

"What was he like?" Dad asked.

"He was a lousy tipper," said the driver.

"That's probably because he didn't understand our money," I said.

"I don't think that was it," said the driver. "I think he was just a lousy tipper."

When we pulled up at Dr. Kropotkin's, Dad gave the driver some money. Then we carefully pulled the creature out from the backseat.

"You tip like you're from outer space," said the driver. Then he drove off.

Dad carried the creature into Dr. Kropotkin's apartment.

"Well, well, well," said Dr. Kropotkin. "Come in, folks. Zack, I haven't seen you in a while."

"No, sir," I said.

"The last time you were in my office, I believe you'd swallowed disappearing ink and were becoming invisible."

"That's right," I said.

"Well, it looks like you've recovered," he said.

"Yes," I said.

"And how did I cure you?" said Dr. Kropotkin. "I don't recall."

"You didn't cure me," I said. "The heat from some TV lights I was standing under made me turn visible again."

"Ah," said Dr. Kropotkin. "So. Whom do we have here? A little friend from school?"

"Nope," I said. "A little friend from outer space."

"Ah. And what seems to be the matter with him?"

"He fainted when he saw us," said Dad.

"Well, let's have a look at him," said the doctor.

Dad carried the creature into the doctor's study. He put the creature down on a leather couch. The doctor shone a light in the creature's eyes. Then he looked in what seemed to be the creature's ear holes. And in what seemed to be the creature's nose. And in what we thought was the creature's mouth. Then the doctor took the creature's pulse.

"I get three hundred forty-seven," said the doctor.

"And that's high, right?" I said.

"For a human, yes," said the doctor. "For a hummingbird, low."

The doctor put his stethoscope on the creature's chest and listened.

"How's his heart?" Dad asked.

"Fine," said the doctor. "Both of them."

The doctor wanted to give the creature a complete exam. We tried to take off the creature's tin-foil suit. There didn't seem to be any buttons or zippers. After a while we found a seam that just peeled open.

"Look at this," said Dad.

The creature was wearing a T-shirt with something written on it.

"What does it say?" asked the doctor.

Dad bent close to look at it.

"It's in some strange language I've never seen before," he said.

Just then the creature's eyes popped open.

Chapter 3

The creature screamed. Or what seemed to be a scream. It actually sounded a lot like yodeling. Then he tried to get up. Dad and Dr. Kropotkin held him down on the table.

"Calm down, little fellow," said Dr. Kropotkin. "We mean you no harm. We're just trying to help you."

"Can...you...understand...what... we...are...saying?" said Dad. Dad spoke very slowly and very loudly.

"Can...you...un-der-*stand*...what... we...are...*say*-ing?" I repeated even louder.

"Please," said the creature in a high, metallic voice. "I may be from another planet—EEP—but I am not *deaf*."

"You speak English!" I said.

"Not precisely," said the creature. "I have—EEP—an omni-speak unit."

"Is that what's making those funny EEP-ing sounds?" I asked.

"Yes," said the creature.

"What the heck is an omni-speak unit?" said Dad.

"A small electronic chip in my mouth. It permits you—EEP—to hear what I say in any language you speak. It permits me to understand—EEP—what *you* say."

"My name is Zack," I said. "This is Dad. And this is Dr. Kropotkin. What's *your* name?"

"BZ7943177568," said the creature. "But you can—EEP—call me BZ for short."

"This is amazing!" said Dad. "An actual

creature from another planet! I didn't even know there was intelligent life on other planets!"

"Well, *I* did not know there was—EEP—intelligent life on *Earth*," said BZ.

"You didn't?" I said. "How could you not know that?"

"One cannot tell from deep space," said BZ. "From deep space, Earth looks—EEP—like a dust bunny. And that is—EEP—on a *good* day."

"What does it say on your T-shirt?" Dad asked.

"It says—EEP—'My leader went to Earth and all he brought me was this lousy T-shirt.' It is a joke, Dad. People on my planet—EEP—do not believe there are T-shirts on Earth."

"Which planet are you from?" I asked.

"In your language—EEP—it would be called Fred."

"You're from the planet Fred?" I said. "Where's that?"

"You hang a left at Venus. You go into hyperspace—EEP—and get off at the first galaxy. We are the seventh planet on the right. You cannot miss it."

"If you didn't know there was intelligent life here," said Dad, "why did you come?"

"My fuel gauge is no longer working, Dad," said BZ. "My fuel was so low—EEP—I was forced to make an emergency landing. Imagine my surprise when I saw a city down here. What is it called, by the way?"

"New York," I said.

"New York?" said BZ. "That is—EEP—a strange name."

"No stranger than calling a planet Fred," I said.

"Good point!" said BZ. "Intelligent—EEP—life on Earth! They are never going to believe this back on Fred. Ho ho!"

"You're low on fuel," I said. "What do you use for fuel in a UFO?"

BZ reached inside his tin-foil suit. He held up a small bottle of something.

"This is what we use," he said. "But my supply—EEP—is now exhausted. I do not suppose you have any of this on Earth, do you?"

He took the top off the bottle and handed it to me. I sniffed it.

"This stuff smells like mayonnaise," I said.

"Let me smell that," said Dad. I handed him the bottle. "Zack is right," he said. "It *does* smell like mayonnaise."

"Let *me* smell that," said Dr. Kropotkin.

Dad handed him the bottle. The doctor sniffed it. Then he dipped his finger in the bottle and licked it. The doctor was a brave man like Dad.

"Yep. It's mayonnaise, all right," said the

doctor. "Hellman's Real Mayonnaise, in fact."

"We can go to the A&P and buy you enough to fly back to Planet Fred," I said.

"Then—EEP—I shall owe you my life," said BZ.

First we went to the A&P and bought eight jars of Hellman's Real Mayonnaise. The giant sized ones. Then we took off for Central Park and the UFO. It was a nice night, so we decided to walk. Lucky Dad is so strong because all those jars were kind of heavy.

When we got to Fifth Avenue, I saw something that gave me the creeps.

"Pssst, Dad," I said. "I think we're being followed."

"By whom?" said Dad.

I pointed.

"See that man and woman in the trench

coats? They're the ones we saw in the park, poking around in the bushes."

Dad turned around. Then he turned back.

"They do look like the same people," he said. "But I don't think they're following us. They're probably just out for a stroll."

"Whatever you say," I said. Then I turned to BZ. "Do you have a long ride home tonight?"

"It is not too long," said BZ. "Only three thousand light-years. That is—EEP—a snap in hyperspace."

"Still," said Dad, "we'd better get you back to your spaceship."

When we got back to Central Park we went right to the place where we'd left the spaceship. But it was gone! Vanished! Erased! Where the spaceship had been there was now only a burned ring in the grass.

Chapter 4

Poor BZ was really upset.

"Where is my spacecraft?" he kept saying over and over again. "What—EEP EEP—has happened to my spacecraft? It wasn't even mine. It was—EEP—a rental. And you know how unpleasant rental companies can be when—EEP—you lose their vehicles."

"While we were at the doctor's, somebody must have stolen it," Dad said.

"Has anything like this ever—EEP—happened before in New York?" asked BZ.

Dad and I looked at each other.

"Every once in a while," I said.

"We'd better find a police station," said Dad.

"Freeze!" said a voice behind us.

We put down our plastic grocery bags, raised our hands, and slowly turned around. There were the man and woman who'd been following us. They both had guns pointed right at us.

"Wh-who are you?" I asked.

"I don't have to tell you. But I will. FBI," said the man. "I'm Special Agent Moldy. And this is Special Agent Scaley. Who are *you*?"

"My name is Zack," I said. "And this is my dad."

"And who is this?" said Moldy. He was pointing to BZ.

"A friend of ours," I said.

"We have reason to believe that one of you is an alien life-form," said Moldy.

"Assuming there *are* such things," said Scaley. "Which I personally doubt."

"Which one of you is the alien life-form?" said Moldy.

Nobody said anything.

"You might as well tell us," said Moldy. "We're going to find out anyway, sooner or later."

"I don't know what you're talking about," said Dad. "Nobody has ever proven there's intelligent life on other planets."

"See?" said Scaley to Moldy. "What have I been telling you?"

Moldy turned to BZ.

"What's your name, fella?" he asked.

"His name is BZ," I said. "He goes to my school. The Horace Hyde-White School for Boys."

"Why don't you let *him* tell me?" said Moldy.

"Tell him, BZ," I said.

"My name—EEP—is BZ," said BZ. "I go to his school. The—EEP—Horace Hyde-White School for Boys."

"That's better," said Moldy. "But what's with the EEPs?"

"He has the hiccups," I said.

Suddenly Moldy pulled out his gun and stuck it in BZ's face.

"FREEZE OR I'LL SHOOT!" shouted Moldy.

Poor BZ fainted again.

"Hiccups gone?" asked Moldy in a friendly tone.

I revived BZ and helped him to his feet.

"I think so," I said.

"Never fails," said Moldy, putting his gun away. "Folks, we have reason to believe there was an alien spacecraft parked here earlier."

"Assuming there *are* such things," said Scaley. "Which I personally doubt."

"You people have any idea where this space vehicle might be now?" Moldy asked.

"Not at all," said Dad.

"I wish we did," I said.

"Yeah?" said Moldy suspiciously. "Why do you wish that?"

"Uh, because we'd really like to see one," I said.

"Yeah," said Moldy. "Me, too. I'm afraid *They* got to it first."

"They?" I asked. "Who are *They*?"

Moldy looked around quickly.

"Let's just say I have reason to believe it's a government conspiracy," he said.

"Oh, Moldy, for crying out loud," said Scaley. "It's not a government conspiracy. You think *everything's* a government conspiracy."

"Everything *is*," said Moldy.

"Let's go, Moldy," said Scaley.

"I'd suggest you not tell anyone we had this little talk," said Moldy. He looked around to make sure nobody overheard us.

"Sorry to have troubled you, folks," said Scaley. "Say, do you need a lift home?"

"No, that's OK," I said.

"Nonsense," said Moldy. "We're not letting you walk through the park alone at night. *They* might abduct you."

"Our car's right over there," said Scaley. "C'mon."

Dad flashed me a worried look. We really needed to find BZ's spacecraft. But we couldn't do that till we got rid of Moldy and Scaley.

"A lift home would be great," said Dad.

We picked up the mayo again and followed agents Moldy and Scaley.

As we walked, BZ leaned toward me and whispered, "You caused me to—EEP—tell an untruth, Zack."

"By saying you go to my school, you mean?"

"And by saying I am a boy."

"What?" I said.

"Zack," said BZ. "Can you not tell that I am—EEP—a Freddian girl?"

Chapter 5

"**W**hoa!" I said. "You're a *girl*?" I could hardly believe my ears.

"And quite a beautiful one," said BZ. "On Planet Fred, all the boys—EEP—are always asking me for dates."

"Uh, cool," I said.

"Hey, guys," Dad called. "Walk a little faster, would you?"

We hurried to the car and got inside. Moldy and Scaley in the front. Dad, BZ, the mayo, and me in the back. Dad gave Moldy our address.

I was still trying to get used to what BZ had told me when she whispered again in my ear, "Zack, do you think I am—EEP—beautiful?"

The last thing I wanted to do was hurt BZ's feelings. I wasn't too sure a girl with no hair, no ears, and a weird nose was beautiful. But I was willing to believe that back on Planet Fred she was a real babe. And people on Fred would probably think Gwyneth Paltrow was a real bow-wow.

"Uh, yeah," I said. "You're beautiful. Definitely."

"I think you are—EEP—beautiful, too," said BZ.

"Thanks," I said.

Then she licked me on the hand. At least I *think* it was a lick. It was wet. It kind of creeped me out, if you want to know the truth. Maybe it was some kind of Freddian gesture of friendship. Like a slap on the back.

Moldy's cell phone rang.

"Agent Moldy," he said, answering. "Right. Really? No kidding. What's that location again? OK. We're on our way."

"What's going on?" Dad asked.

"An alien spacecraft has been spotted at the north end of the park," said Moldy. "We're going to investigate. I hope you folks don't mind tagging along."

Dad, BZ, and I were very excited. We'd never have been able to find BZ's spacecraft on our own.

"We don't mind tagging along at all," said Dad.

"Neither do I," said BZ innocently. "I have always wanted to see—EEP—what an alien spacecraft looks like up close."

Chapter 6

In ten minutes we reached the north end of the park. Up ahead, just beyond the trees, we saw something. A weird glow in the sky. Searchlights.

"That must be it!" said Moldy excitedly. "This is an important moment for me, Scaley. I'm finally going to see my first UFO!"

He pulled the car to a stop beside some trees and parked. Moldy and Scaley took their guns out of their holsters.

"You people stay here," said Scaley.

"Right," said Dad.

But as soon as Moldy and Scaley walked through the trees, we followed. BZ grabbed my hand in the darkness. She had quite a grip.

"BZ," I said. "I'm going to need that hand back."

"Why?" she said.

"Because any minute now, I'm going to have to scratch my nose."

"Scratch—EEP—with your other hand," she said.

As we followed Moldy and Scaley toward the weird searchlight glow, we noticed something else up ahead. A metallic Frisbee-shaped thing hovering over the trees. A UFO? BZ and I walked faster. Then, just ahead of us, Moldy and Scaley burst out of the trees and into a big clearing, guns out. We followed.

What we saw was a carnival. A Ferris wheel. A merry-go-round. A roller coaster, with cars in the shape of rockets. A stand that sold cotton candy. And there, on top of a giant crane, was a UFO.

Well, maybe not a real UFO. And certainly not BZ's UFO. It was a round, Frisbee-shaped, cheesy-looking thing that looked a little like BZ's. But not much. It had a big sign on it: GENUINE UFO FROM OUTER SPACE! NOT A FAKE! THIS IS THE REAL DEAL! ADULTS RIDE $1.00, KIDS 50¢! YOU MUST BE AT LEAST AS TALL AS THIS SIGN TO COMMAND THIS ALIEN SPACECRAFT!

Moldy and Scaley just stood there. Guns out. Looking stupid. People were staring nervously at them. Finally Scaley put her gun away.

"I have never been so embarrassed in my entire life," she said.

"Yes, you have," said Moldy, putting his gun away. "Just yesterday. Remember?"

"Oh, right," said Scaley.

We walked back to where we'd parked the car. But the car was gone.

"Oh, poop!" said Scaley. She kicked the dirt.

"What happened to your car?" I asked.

"Stolen, obviously," said Scaley. She turned to Moldy. "Will you at least admit to me there's no such thing as a UFO?" she asked.

"Here's what I believe," said Moldy. "I believe *They* heard we were coming. I believe *They* replaced the real UFO with the fake one we saw. *They* were following us, and as soon as we got out of the car, *They* stole it. It's a conspiracy, Scaley. Just as I've always thought."

Scaley slapped her forehead.

"Moldy, you are absolutely bonkers!" shrieked Scaley. "You are absolutely out of your mind! There is no conspiracy! There are no alien spacecraft! There are no little green men from outer space!" She turned to us. "Am I right, or am I wrong?"

"Well," I said. "I've never seen any little green *men*."

"See?" said Scaley. "Even this ten-year-old *kid* has more sense than you do!"

Chapter
7

Moldy and Scaley stomped off into the dark, looking for their car and yelling at each other.

"I am very upset—EEP—that my spaceship is gone," said BZ. "There will be—EEP—terrible late charges from the rental company."

"We're going to find it for you, BZ," I said.

I don't know why I said that. I didn't have a clue where BZ's spaceship was. I just wanted to make her feel better.

I remembered there's a police station in Central Park. They always help out with missing vehicles...although usually ones manufactured on this planet. With me leading the way, Dad, BZ and I walked to the Central Park Precinct. We marched right up to the sergeant behind the desk.

"Officer, we'd like to report a stolen vehicle," said Dad.

"OK," said the desk sergeant. He started filling out a form. "What was the make and year of the vehicle?"

I could see we were heading for trouble.

"I don't know," said my Dad.

"You don't know?" said the desk sergeant.

"No," said Dad.

I pulled on Dad's arm. "Uh, maybe we should leave."

"How could you not know?" said the desk sergeant. "Doesn't the vehicle belong to you?"

"Not me," said Dad. He pointed to BZ. "Him."

"Him?" said the desk sergeant. "He looks a little young to drive. How old are you, son?"

"Seventy-one parludes," said BZ.

"Excuse me?" said the desk sergeant, and he gave BZ a puzzled look. Then he said in a tired voice, "Just give me your license and registration."

"My what?" said BZ.

"He, uh, may not have the kind of license and registration you'd recognize," said Dad.

"He from out of state?" said the desk sergeant.

"Yes, sir," said Dad. "*Way* out of state."

The desk sergeant stuck out his hand. "Papers, please."

BZ seemed confused. But she reached into her tin-foil suit and brought out a little rolled-up something. She unrolled it. It was a clear plastic sheet. Like Saran Wrap, only heavier. It had lots of writing on it. It looked like the writing on her T-shirt. She handed it to the desk sergeant.

The desk sergeant squinted at the clear plastic sheet. "OK, show me where it says the make and year of the car."

"It wasn't exactly a car," said my dad.

"What was it, a motorcycle?"

"Not exactly," said Dad.

"Then what was it?"

"It was a more a...a spacecraft," I said. I really thought it was a mistake being here. But then the desk sergeant said, "A spacecraft? Wait a minute. Was that the round thing parked just off the Sheep Meadow, behind the trees?"

"You mean you saw it?" I said excitedly.

"We saw it, all right," said the desk

sergeant. "It was illegally parked. We had it towed."

"Towed?" I said. "Towed where?"

"Where we tow all illegally parked vehicles in New York," said the desk sergeant. "Pier 76. On Thirty-eighth Street and the Hudson River." He handed back the clear plastic sheet. "I suggest you go down there and pick it up as soon as possible. And it's going to cost you a bundle."

Chapter 8

The Department of Motor Vehicles clerk at Pier 76 had a beard and wore a beanie. Right away he started filling out a long Department of Transportation form.

"I want my spaceship back," said BZ.

"Sshhhh," I said.

"License and registration," said the clerk without looking up.

"BZ, give him your license and registration," Dad said.

BZ unrolled her sheet of plastic. The

clerk took it and studied it closely. Then he began copying the strange symbols from BZ's roll of plastic onto his form. I guess he had seen other crazy registrations before. After a long time of filling out the form, he looked up again.

"One hundred seventy-five dollars, please," he said. "No checks or credit cards."

"Wow," said Dad.

"What—EEP—does he say?" asked BZ.

"He says the fine for parking is a hundred and seventy-five dollars," said Dad.

"Is that—EEP—much money?" asked BZ.

"Yeah," I said.

"BZ," said Dad. "You wouldn't happen to have any money, would you?"

"Oh—EEP—certainly," said BZ. "I always carry money."

"Thank heavens," said Dad.

BZ reached into her tin-foil suit and

plunked something down on the counter. It was a diamond about the size of a bubble gum ball.

"I cannot make change for this," said the clerk. "Do you have anything smaller?"

"I am sorry," said BZ.

Dad took some bills out of his pocket and counted them.

"I've got exactly a hundred and seventy-one dollars," Dad said. "That's four dollars short."

"They won't give back BZ's spacecraft unless the fine is paid," I said.

"And they don't take checks or credit cards," said Dad. "What do we do now?"

I dumped out my pockets. In one I had a piece of Dubble-Bubble and an unwrapped sticky cough drop. In another I had two crumpled-up dollar bills and a bunch of coins. I counted out the coins. I had more than two dollars in change.

"I have four dollars and thirteen cents," I said. "With what Dad has, we've got the fine, plus an extra thirteen cents."

"Great," said Dad.

Dad handed the clerk his hundred and seventy-one dollars. I gave the clerk my four dollars.

Then BZ gave Dad her diamond.

"BZ," said Dad. "I can't take this."

"It is—EEP—not necessary to make change," said BZ. "You have been very kind to me. Please, keep the change."

"But this diamond is worth thousands of dollars," said Dad. "I couldn't possibly take it from you."

"Unless you take it, I shall—EEP—be very insulted," said BZ.

"Well," said Dad, "only if you're sure."

"I am sure," said BZ.

The clerk marked the fine paid. Then a man in blue coveralls led us back to the outdoor parking lot and showed us where they'd put BZ's spacecraft. The spacecraft wasn't glowing anymore. And it wasn't floating three feet off the ground.

"Aha!" said a voice behind us. "I thought you said you didn't know anything about alien spacecraft."

We turned around. Agents Moldy and Scaley were standing right behind us.

"Hey," I said. "What are you doing here?"

Moldy and Scaley looked a little embarrassed. "Actually," said Moldy. "it turned out that *They* didn't steal our car after all. It was towed. But don't change the subject. Whose alien spacecraft is this?"

"This isn't an alien spacecraft," I said. "It's BZ's car. It's a rental."

"See?" said Scaley to Moldy.

"I've never seen a car like *that* before," said Moldy.

"It's a foreign job," said Dad.

"Oh, I see," said Moldy. He seemed disappointed. "You *sure* it's not an alien spacecraft?"

"Pretty sure," said Dad.

"Oh, Moldy, for crying out loud," said Scaley. "It's not an alien spacecraft, OK?"

"And what makes you so sure?" asked Moldy.

"I happen to be a doctor, OK?" said Scaley.

"Right," said Moldy. "OK then. By the way, what kind of mileage do you get on this baby?" he asked BZ.

"What does he ask about babies?" said BZ.

"He wants to know how far you can go on a gallon of fuel," I said.

"About—EEP—two thousand light-years per gallon," said BZ.

"Is that city driving, or highway?" asked Moldy.

"Highway," I said.

"What do you use, regular gas or premium?" asked Moldy.

"Mayonnaise," said BZ before I could stop her.

"Mayonnaise?" said Moldy. He was frowning. "You know, now that you mention it, there are eight jumbo jars of Hellman's Real Mayonnaise in the backseat of my car. They wouldn't happen to be yours, would they?"

"Actually, they are," I told him. I'd forgotten all about them.

"Oh good," said Moldy, his frown gone. "That's another case solved! I thought maybe it was a case of psychic teleportation."

We got the mayonnaise out of the car,

then agents Moldy and Scaley said good-bye. Moldy put one hand on my shoulder and one on BZ's. "Remember, kids," he said in a serious voice, "the truth is out there."

"Of course—EEP—it is," BZ said.

Moldy and Scaley got in their car, arguing the whole time. And that was the last I saw of them. Sometimes I wonder if Moldy ever did find proof of alien life.

"It is time for me to return to my planet," said BZ. "May I give you—EEP—a ride to your home?"

"Seeing as how we have only thirteen cents left," said Dad, "that might be a good idea. If it's not out of your way."

"No no, it is—EEP—in the same direction as Venus," said BZ.

Chapter 9

On Monday I told the kids in school.

"There's no such things as UFO's," said Vernon Manteuffel. He doesn't know anything. Also, he sweats a lot.

"There may be intelligent life on other planets," said my best friend, Spencer. "But there's no evidence it has ever visited Earth."

The only person who believed me was Andrew Clancy, the kid who's always trying to top me.

"I think Zack's telling the truth," said Andrew.

"You do?" said Spencer.

"Sure," said Andrew. "There *is* intelligent life on other planets. And space creatures *have* visited Earth. In fact, I was on board a UFO myself. And it was a whole lot bigger than the one Zack was on, I can tell you that."

OK, so no one really believed me. But they sure had trouble explaining where Dad and I got that 143 karat diamond!

What else happens to Zack?
Find out in

Evil Queen Tut and the Great Ant Pyramids

I looked around. And then I noticed something else that was strange. The bushes and trees on all sides of me seemed to be growing. What was going on here?

And then it hit me: My clothes weren't getting bigger. *I was getting smaller!* A lot smaller. I was shrinking fast, like a pat of butter in a hot frying pan.

Before I knew it, I was no more than a foot high. I couldn't believe it. A minute ago I was a normal-sized boy. Now I was the size of a chihuahua. And I was still shrinking!